A Picture Book for Grown-Ups

-Ben Joel Price-

Skyhorse Publishing

In loving memory
of Jack and Jim.

You would have both died laughing.

Acknowledgments
The author would like to thank
all things that go bump in the night.

Disclaimer
All trick-or-treaters appearing in
this book were harmed during the
time of writing.

Knock knock...
there's some bodies at the door.

No.

-12-

Twelve Trick-or-Treaters
On a fateful jaunt,
Woe betide the victims
Of their nasty little haunt.

A rotten little robot
By the name of Rusty Glitch
Malfunctioned rather badly
In a game of Ding, Dong, Ditch.

The door bell was the culprit;
A botch job wrongly wired,
And unfortunately for Rusty,
His warranty's now expired.

No.

-11-

Eleven Trick-or-Treaters
TP-ing up the 'burbs,
Oblivious to the warning signs
They continue undeterred.

A musty little mummy
By the name of Ackrid Sprat
Was the next unlucky guiser
Whose evening fell rather flat.

An accident waiting to happen
Put a stop to Ackrid's tricks,
As now they're buried with her
Under a pyramid of bricks.

No.

-10-

Ten Trick-or-Treaters
Shrugging off the fear,
They're being picked off one by one
But still they persevere.

A crooked little critter
By the name of Heskith Dregs
Was decorating cabin 10
With a dozen rotten eggs.

He failed to hear the patter
of a thousand tiny feet.
There really wasn't anything
they didn't like to eat.

No.

- 9 -

Nine Trick-or-Treaters
Making quite a din,
Teasing the local junkyard dog,
Its temperament wearing thin.

A scrawny little skeleton
By the name of Crocus Munge
Was the next annoying trickster
To be savagely expunged.

Dragged right through the pet flap
Her chances were pretty slim.
She was licked from head to toe
And ravaged limb from limb.

No.

- 8 -

Eight Trick-or-Treaters
Creeping through the farm.
They tried to steal some apples
But they've triggered the alarm.

An obnoxious little oculus
By the name of Orville Snide,
Was safe in his secret hiding place...
Until he went and cried.

Trapped with reeking onions
It's as bad as Orville fears,
For now it's him who's bobbing
As he drowns in his own tears.

No.

-7-

Seven Trick-or-Treaters
Pranking through the night,
Rupturing gobs of flour bombs
On all they choose to smite.

A cranky little circus clown
By the name of Frisby Dent
Mistook the drapes at No.7
For a traveling circus tent.

Engulfed in the fumigation
A hideous thing occurred,
She spewed her own intestines,
And now the joke's on her.

No.

-6-

Six Trick-or-Treaters
With an explosive box of tricks.
Fire crackers and cherry bombs
Is how they get their kicks.

A twisted little tiki
By the name of Jonty Zoph
May have still been with us
If he hadn't been showing off.

He lit the whole caboodle
In thinking it'd be fun,
Creating a mass inferno
Leaving him crispy and "well done."

No.

-5-

Five Trick-or-Treaters
Stealing other children's treats,
The street is now on lockdown
But the curfew has been breached.

A manic little martian
By the name of Xanthe Blight
Was drawn to the door at No. 5
By an alluring beam of light.

Curiosity got the better of her,
Which really was a shame;
She climbed aboard the alien ship
And was never seen again.

No.

-4-

Four Trick-or-Treaters
Smashing window panes.
Each protest their innocence
But someone is to blame.

An irksome little insect
By the name of Brundle Coop,
Had overstayed his welcome
Buzzing on the Jones's stoop.

They called upon the swat team
Causing Brundle much distress,
As 40 seconds later
They disposed of the little pest.

PRIVATE
PROPERTY
TRESPASSING IS
ENCOURAGED

3

CRONE

No.

-3-

Three Trick-or-Treaters
Now anticipate the worst.
They're beginning to get the feeling
That their futures may be cursed.

A wretched little wicked witch
By the name of Nettely Shrill
Had baked a batch of "Bug-ins"*
For the ladies on the hill.

* "Bug-ins"—six-legged muffins

She invited herself for supper
To which the coven much obliged.
They showed her to the oven,
And then bundled her inside.

No.

-2-

Two Trick-or-Treaters
Soaking passersby,
They've finally been rewarded
With some sugary supplies.

A malodorous little merman
By the name of Gurnard Seep
Smelled something rather fishy
Before he plunged into the deep.

As he sank he realized
He'd been a fool to take the bait,
Which gave him little comfort
In accepting his own fate.

No.

-1-

One Trick-or-Treater
At an undisclosed address,
Whose twisted tricks had worked a treat—
The night's been a success.

This sinister little shadow
Whose name remains unknown,
Climbs aboard a ferryboat
And begins its journey home.

It glides back down to the underworld
Through a dark and eerie hole.
There's no candy in its bag of treats,
Just 11 unfortunate souls.

Ben Joel Price lives!...
and creates from an old victorian house in London.
He is the author-illustrator of children's books,
Earth Space Moon Base and *In The Deep Dark Deep*
as well as a tasty little morsel called *Love bites*.
This is his fourth book. You can visit him at
www.benjoelprice.com

His top five notable fears are:
1.Great White Sharks!
(a self diagnosed selachophobe, still blames *Jaws*)
2.Over crowding
3.Audience participation
4.Doors that are difficult to open
5.That thing that lives in the cupboard